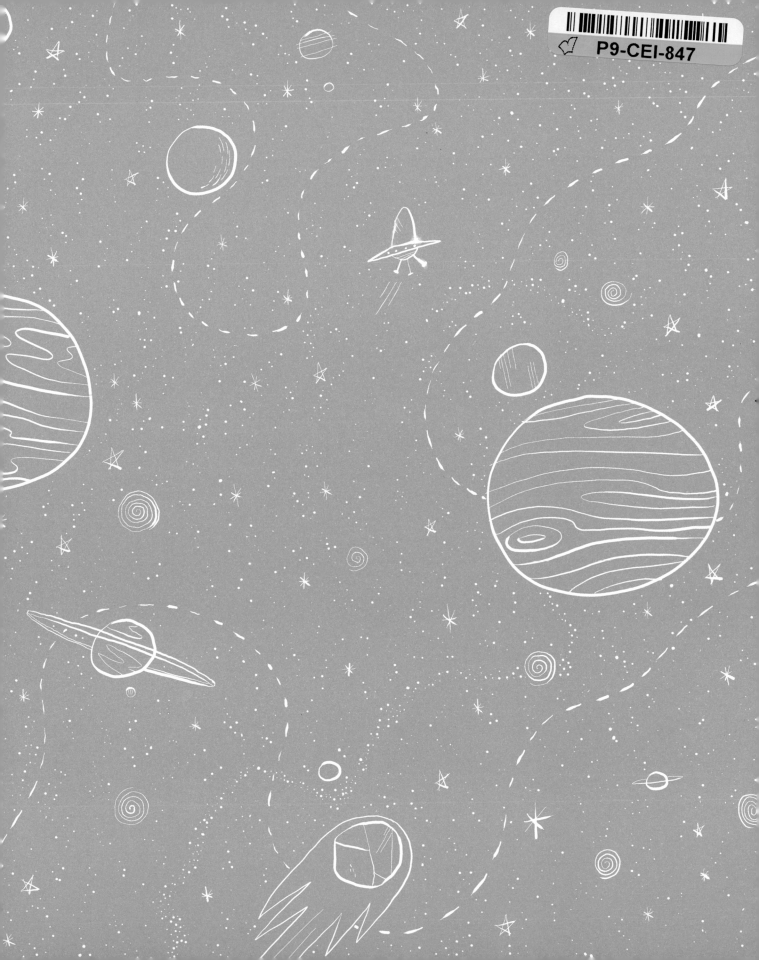

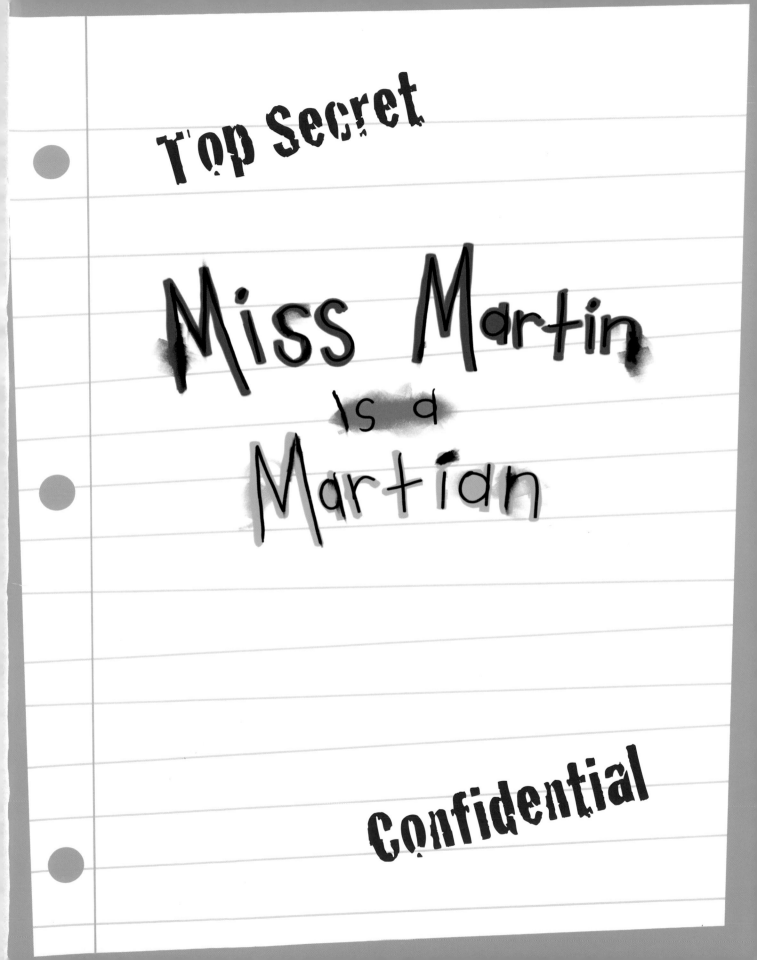

To Ernie, an extraordinary educator and friend.
—C.F.

To my mom and dad, who are not aliens as far as I know.
—J.C.

Miss Martin Is a Martian
Text Copyright © 2011 by Colleen Murray Fisher
Illustration Copyright © by 2011 Jared Chapman

A Mackinac Island Book
Published by Charlesbridge
85 Main Street
Watertown, MA 02472
(617) 926-0329
www.charlesbridge.com

Library of Congress Cataloging-in-Publication Data on file

Fiction

ISBN 978-1-934133-38-5 (hardcover)
ISBN 978-1-934133-39-2 (paperback)

Summary: Melvin Eugene Baxter is convinced now more than ever that his new teacher, Miss Martin, is a Martian.

Layout and Design by Tom Mills

Manufactured by Regent Publishing Services, Hong Kong
Printed March 2011 in Heyuan, Guangdong, China

(hc) 10 9 8 7 6 5 4 3 2 1
(sc) 10 9 8 7 6 5 4 3 2 1

Miss Martin
Is a
Martian

by Colleen Murray Fisher

illustrated by Jared Chapman

Mackinac Island Press

for the love of reading

After watching MARTIANS INVADE MICHIGAN at the movies this weekend, I'm more convinced now than ever that my new teacher, Miss Martin, IS A **MARTIAN;** and that I, Melvin Eugene Baxter, will have to make it my mission to STOP HER BEFORE SHE TAKES OVER THE PLANET.

Miss Martin →

Miss Martin as an Alien ←

In case something should happen to me, I will document my findings in my journal so that the WHOLE WORLD WILL KNOW THE TRUTH before

IT'S TOO LATE.

WEDNESDAY, SEPTEMBER 8

Today I observed Miss Martin's Martian powers in action. During our healthy snack time, I was very sneaky and extra careful to dispose of the evidence, but Miss Martin was still able to detect that I ate a chocolate cupcake.

The ONLY WAY she could have known is if she used her superior sense of **SMELL,** which everyone knows Martians possess.

Tomorrow I will have to **TEST**
Miss Martin's powers out on
Chocolate Chip Cookies.

THURSDAY, SEPTEMBER 9

Like all Martians, Miss Martin

HAS EYES IN THE BACK OF HER HEAD.

I can't see them because her hair covers them
up, but I know they exist because today during
art I wanted to see if orange crayons actually
TASTE LIKE ORANGES, and my friend Billy
thought the glue looked rather appetizing.

Even though Miss Martin was facing the chalkboard the whole time, she figured out our taste-testing experiment and told us to never try it again.

The only thing we figured out is that orange crayons taste nothing like oranges, and that IT IS POSSIBLE TO GLUE YOUR MOUTH SHUT.

FRIDAY, SEPTEMBER 10

I MADE AN IMPORTANT DISCOVERY TODAY that not even someone with my SUPREME KNOWLEDGE of Martian life could have known. When Billy and I came out of the bathroom, Miss Martin reminded us, "Good character means doing the right thing even when no one is looking."

The only way Miss Martin could have known we were playing around in the bathroom is if Martians have the power to see through walls. I wonder if the "eyes in the back of their heads"

HAVE X-RAY VISION TOO.

NOTE TO SELF:
Remember not to wear my polka-dotted underwear to school tomorrow.

MONDAY, SEPTEMBER 13

In social studies class today, I learned that
MISS MARTIN HAS A SUPERHUMAN, or should I say a
SUPER-MARTIAN, MEMORY.

She mentioned that she knows the names of all fifty
states and their capitals. She also said that if we study
really hard, one day we will know them all just like her.

Only a **MARTIAN** would be able to remember all that junk, and there is no way on Earth she is going to make me LEARN HER MARTIAN WAYS. After all, I already know that the name of my state is "Michigan" and that the capital of Michigan is "M." Everything I need to know about capitals and lowercase letters I ALREADY LEARNED FROM MY KINDERGARTEN TEACHER (who my mother says is an Earthling).

Capital

Michigan

TUESDAY, SEPTEMBER 14

TODAY I DISCOVERED Miss Martin's plan

TO TAKE OVER THE HUMAN RACE:

she is going to fill our brains with so many new things

that one day soon all of our heads will **EXPLODE!**

Then she will replace them with Martian heads.

Before   After

check list for take over!

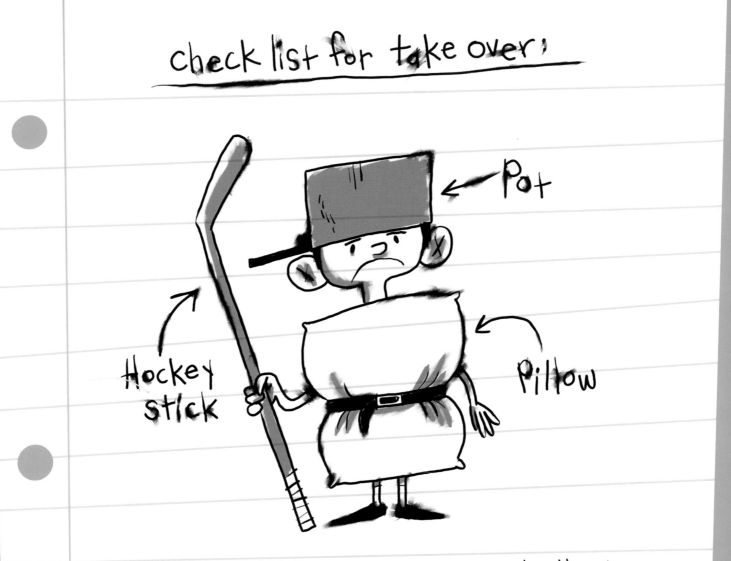

I don't think mine will explode because my brother is always telling me I HAVE EXTRA SPACE IN MY HEAD. I'm not sure what he means by this, but he must know what he's talking about because he's in middle school. So, I think I am safe -- at least for the time being. I just hope I can save the others before their heads go flying off (EVEN THOUGH THAT WOULD BE REALLY COOL TO SEE).

WEDNESDAY, SEPTEMBER 15

While walking by Miss Martin's desk, I saw a note written in **MARTIANESE.** It looked like a valuable piece of evidence, so I asked Billy, my research assistant, to examine it. Billy thought it might be CURSIVE WRITING, but I reminded him that we don't learn cursive writing until third grade, and Miss Martin is a second grade teacher so she hasn't learned it yet either.

THURSDAY, SEPTEMBER 16

I'm afraid Miss Martin is using her

MARTIAN POWERS TO BRAINWASH THE CLASS.

All the kids really like her, and whenever she tells the

class to do something in that sweet Martian voice of

hers, they always do it. She may be able to fool the class,

but MY BRAIN IS TOO SMART TO BE WASHED

(I don't think it even likes soap).

I certainly don't want Miss Martin to know I am on to her "Martian games," so I will have to keep pretending that I think she is a wonderful teacher. I know I can do it, but it won't be easy.

FRIDAY, SEPTEMBER 17

I have questioned my classmates, and I have concluded that NO ONE HAS SEEN Miss Martin go in or out of the bathroom at all during the first two weeks of school. Martians must have the power to hold it for a very, very long time, or maybe they don't have to use the bathroom at all. That's one **MARTIAN POWER I WISH I HAD!**

My research also indicates that Miss Martin is in the classroom before we arrive at school each day, and she never seems to leave after school is over.

This can only mean one thing:

HER SPACESHIP IS LOCATED SOMEWHERE IN THIS SCHOOL.

My guess is that it's hiding in the one place where no student has ever gone before --

THE TEACHERS' LOUNGE!

MONDAY, SEPTEMBER 20

This morning, Miss Martin passed out

SPARKLY NEW PENCILS.

Jason Daniels said, "These are out of this world!"

and I was like, "YEAH, NO KIDDING!" When the

box came to me, I thought it would be best if

I took two -- one for use at school and one for

conducting laboratory testing on at home.

Take only one...

Before I could take the
second pencil,
Miss Martin used her
MARTIAN POWERS
to read my mind and said,
"TAKE ONLY ONE AND
PASS THE BOX AROUND."
I don't want a Martian reading
my mind any more, so I'd better
be more careful and not think at
school ever again.

TUESDAY, SEPTEMBER 21

Everyone knows that **MARTIANS** HAVE EXTRA, INVISIBLE HANDS, and Miss Martin is no exception. Today in math class, she said that 18 + 4 = 22. I did the math, and no matter how hard I tried, I kept running out of fingers and toes to count. I told my assistant about her extra pair of invisible hands, but Billy thought she probably just had an extra toe on each foot.

I guess the only way to figure out which one of us is right is to try to get her to take off her shoes, but I fear that **MARTIAN FOOT ODOR** may be too powerful for Earthlings to handle, and I for one DON'T WANT TO BE RESPONSIBLE FOR HUMAN EXTINCTION.

WEDNESDAY, SEPTEMBER 22

It's really too bad that I'm going to have to take Miss Martin down and expose her secret to the rest of the world, because **MARTIANS**  **SURE DO HAVE A WAY OF MAKING LEARNING FUN.**

Today in science class, I was SO EXCITED TO ANSWER A QUESTION that when I raised my hand, I fell off my chair and bumped my head.

Miss Martin came rushing over and wrapped her arms around me. She used her healing powers that **MARTIANS** learn at MARTIAN SCHOOL to make me feel better. My tears even disappeared! I'll bet she used those invisible hands of hers to wipe them away.

I guess EVERYONE NEEDS a Martian as a teacher every now and then.

THURSDAY, SEPTEMBER 23

After staying up late to read my comic books
last night, I didn't think I would be able to
stay awake in class today, but the minute
I walked into the classroom, Miss Martin put me
in a trance. No matter how hard I fought, her powers
proved too great for me. I couldn't control myself.
I WANTED TO LEARN ALL KINDS OF NEW THINGS.

At silent reading time, I finally put all the pieces of the puzzle together and was able to complete my investigation with a little help from my comic book research.

= Not Martian

I now know that Miss Martin didn't travel to Earth to study intelligent life forms like me, and she didn't come to take over the planet. Miss Martin isn't even a Martian after all. BOY! DID SHE HAVE ME FOOLED!

It's obvious that she is a

SUPERHERO FROM SATURN,

but Miss Martin has
no need to fear.
HER SECRET IS SAFE WITH ME!

Colleen Murray Fisher was raised in Marlette, Michigan—a small city with a big heart. She is an elementary teacher in Livonia and resides in White Lake, Michigan with her husband, Jason, and their two children, Sofie and Sam. She also wrote and illustrated a children's book entitled *The One and Only Bernadette P. McMullen*.

Jared Chapman graduated from both Texas A&M University and the Savannah College of Art and Design (SCAD) and was able to pursue his dream of becoming an animator. Through his observation of other artists he became obsessed with illustrators and once he graduated from SCAD his own obsession with illustration segued him into his own illustration career. Jared, along with his family, calls Austin, Texas, home.